This book belongs to

Gav
....

the **World's Greatest**
Dad

Put a photo
of your own
dad here.

→

Written by Kath Smith
Illustrated by Jacqueline East
Designed by Chris Fraser at Page to Page

This is a Parragon Book
First published in 2005

Parragon
Queen Street House
4 Queen Street
Bath BA1 1HE, UK

ISBN 1-40544-719-2

Printed in China

World's Greatest Dad

Written by Kath Smith ❖ Illustrated by Jacqueline East

When I grow up, I want to be just like my dad.

This is my dad. He says he likes to get up early.

We have important things to read.

He's GREAT!

My dad knows how to do everything. He taught me to ride my bike, to swim and fly a kite.

Dad can run as fast as I can pedal.

This is me and Scruffy doing doggy paddle.

Dad is great at untying knots, too.

He's even teaching me to use a camera!

Here's a photo I took of Dad...he thought I was going to drop the camera...but I didn't!

My dad is big and strong. He can build anything.
He's smart, too.

Dad can carry lots of things all at once.

And he always shows me how to
do a job properly.

But even Dad needs the instructions!

Scruffy ran off with the instructions, so Dad had to guess how to put up the tent.

I like helping my dad do jobs. And he likes it when I help him.

Dad says I was smart to get the instructions off Scruffy...

...and spot that there was a peg missing from our tent.

Together, we're a great team!

I always feel safe when my dad is in charge...

Dad says you can never be too careful. That's why he always does the barbecue.

...because he always knows what to do.

One of the sausages caught fire, so Dad dunked it in the water bucket.

I made some warning signs for our barbecue party. Can you guess what they mean?

My dad is a fantastic cook, too.

Dad cooks plenty of food for everyone - even for Scruffy.

Everybody loves his Barbecue Sausage Surprise!

My friends and I have great fun with my dad...

I think Dad's favourite game is horse rides.

... and he NEVER gets tired.

Everyone wants another go!

It's my friends' favourite game, too.

Dad invents lots of brilliant games.

Dad invented Paper Plate Chase...

...and Bun-ball!

Dad's team	My team
卌 |||	卌	
	卌 |||

He NEVER runs out of ideas!

Nothing is too difficult if my dad's there to help me.

Dad hit the ball so hard, it got stuck in a tree...

...but we rescued it!

He makes me feel like I'm on top of the world!

It's sad when my friends go home. But sometimes it's great when it's just my dad and me.

EVERYONE said it was a brilliant barbecue party.

He's always joking around!

When we took down the tent, my dad got stuck inside - Scruffy thought he was a monster!

At the end of the day, Dad says we deserve a rest...

We cleared up two slices of chocolate cake.
Scruffy had the left-over sausages.

...but not until we've cleared up.

I hope I grow up to be just like my dad...

...because he's the World's Greatest Dad!